THE CONTINUING SAGA OF RIKKI TIKKI TAVI

STORY BY LaDENE M. HAYES

WRITTEN BY LaDENE M. HAYES

ILLUSTRATIONS BY JAY W

BOOK THREE

FOREWORD

LaDene, the author of this book, is my sister-in-law. As a self-published author myself, I was honored when she asked me to write the foreword to her third installation of the highly dramatic tale: The Continuing Saga of Rikki Tikki Tavi. Her courage to go after her dream as an author has inspired and motivated me, as well as others, to remain dedicated to our crafts. As a senior citizen, she has demonstrated time and time again that pursuing one's heart's desires never gets old.

LaDene's ability to paint word-pictures dates way back to her childhood. Growing up in the early 1950's in a family of nine with only one income, times were sometimes a bit hard. But if you ask LaDene if she was poor as a child, she would say, "No." She was rich in her imagination and creativity. She used them to entertain her younger siblings as well as herself. Unlike some adults, LaDene's childlike imagination only grew with the passing years. This book is truly a manifestation of those skills.

As I read each volume of The Continuing Saga of Rikki Tikki Tavi, I was visually entertained by the colorful animated characters that seemed to move across the pages. Her telling of the stories made them actually come alive for me. The mystery, excitement and intrigue of the storylines of each book made me anxious to turn the pages to see what would happen next. At the end of each volume, I waited impatiently for the publication of its sequel. Finally, it came and I was never disappointed as each one was packed with more and more drama.

Like me, you will not be able to get enough as you turn the pages of The Continuing Saga of Rikki Tikki Tavi written by LaDene M. Hayes.

Herbert W. Davis

In Loving Memory of and dedicated to and special thanks to:

Grant Ruffin Hayes, Jr. (beloved brother), Theressa Thigpen,
Valerie Roy, James "Red" Timmons, Debra Harrison (dear friends),
James and Herbert Hayes (precious uncles), Angela, Sheila, and
Lorraine Gladden (1st cousins), and "Mom" Annie Roberts.

Dedicated to Haley Daria and special thanks to Jay W.

Acknowledgements

I want to thank the Most High Yah for the inspiration and courage to write this book under His instructions and for all He has done for me and continues to do according to (Matt 7:7 and Phil 4:13).

I thank my husband, Glendon Wiggins, for always being a light for me when things seemed dark, Pastors Anthony and Patricia Douglas and the 7th Day Harvest ministry.

I thank everyone for their support on this project and pray they enjoy it.

Thank you!

PROLOGUE

Rikki learns the most dreadful thing that could happen to him has happened! He discovers Lethalee has moved into her parents' destroyed den and has been living there for who knows how long! He learns that it was a rumor that Lethalee was about to lay her own clutch of eggs and that he has to find out the truth about her plans. His greatest fear is that Lethalee might know he is soon to become a father and that his wife and family are in danger!

THIS IS THE CONTINUING SAGA
OF RIKKI TIKKI TAVI

Part 1

LETHALEE

Lethalee looked up and stared into the waterfall. She felt as if she was being watched. But that was impossible. No one knew this entrance but her because this was her own personal hideout. Lethalee surmised that if her aunt and uncle knew about the old tunnels, then others probably did too. With that in mind, she recruited help to reroute new tunnels and plug up the old ones. It took over a year to do it, but she was adamant. Upon completion, she swore the helpers to silence. She wanted to make sure no one knew how to get to Nag's den but her... and one other. Yet, Lethalee felt she was being watched: and just as quickly, the feeling passed. Lethalee settled down and continued to sun.

Introduction

Rikki's eyes were as red as hot coals as he backed out ever so slowly t he way he had come. He had to get away fast because the urge to battle was in his blood, but the time was not yet right!

Part 2

RIKKI

As soon as he was safely distanced from the waterfall and Lethalee, Rikki screamed to the top of his lungs with his war cry and battle dance. "Tik! Tik! Tik!" Louder and louder he screamed with full force while assimilating battle positions and attacks of aggression. Had anyone seen him from a distance, they may have thought Rikki was fighting an invisible opponent. Rikki's eyes were fiery red. His blood boiling with rage, anger, surprise but most of all fear. Yes, fear. Rikki was afraid of what he had just learned!

The daughter of his greatest enemies is alive! The daughter of the king cobras Nag and Nagaena that he killed two years ago lives! She had somehow managed to move back into their den without him knowing. Worst of all, she probably knew all about him; whereas, he did not know a thing about her!

"Oh Rikki," he thought, after all the rage was spent, "You must find out all you can about Lethalee as soon as possible and you must get inside Nag's den to do it!"

Rikki found his way back to the entrance of Nag's den. Closer inspection revealed the dirt had indeed been disturbed and repacked to look as if it had not been opened. Rikki started to dig out the dirt but stopped as he heard Rachel calling him.

"That is Rachel!" Rikki thought. He had forgotten all about her. "Oh no! I must not let her find me here. I never told her about the birthmark on one of the cobras we killed or about Lethalee. I cannot risk upsetting her or making her worry. I have to do this on my own and pray she does not suspect anything."
RIKKI!

Part 3

RACHEL

Rachel felt the warmth of Rikki's body evaporate from her own as he quietly left her side. She assumed he was making a nature call and soon went back to sleep. However, the sun had begun to warm the den and Rachel woke to find Rikki had not returned.

"That is strange," she thought. "Rikki should have been back by now. Surely, he would not go on his rounds without me or at least kiss me good-bye. Well, he can not be far. I will prepare breakfast and if he is not back by the time it is done, I shall go look for him," Rachel decided.

It did not take Rachel long to prepare breakfast. "Rikki! Rikki! Breakfast is ready! Come and get it!" Rachel called. Almost instantly, Rikki dashed in, quite out of breath and hoped that Rachel did not notice that he had dirt in his hand behind his back that came from Nag's den when he had started digging.

Part 4

LETHALEE

She was feeling so relaxed, full, warm and refreshed after consuming such a delicious breakfast of several bird eggs and a small quail. "Hunting is good and I shall enjoy living here when I start a family," she thought to herself.

The lull of the water falling to the rocks below surrounded by the lush green grass was paradise as Lethalee compared it to how the death of Rikki Tikki Tavi would be.

Yes, she was feeling very satisfied with the way things were falling into place. She had accomplished what others had tried. She had lived right under Rikki's nose and he did not even know it! She had moved into her parents' den and he had no clue! She knew all about him while he knew nothing about her! Soon, the perfect opportunity would present itself and she would strike! With Rikki's distraction of pending fatherhood, Lethalee knew it would be the sweetest victory ever!

Lethalee looked in the direction of a faint rustle in the grass to see the green blades swaying gently and separating slowly. With head high and hood spread, Lethalee watched as the large, black head bearing the yellow fang birthmark of the Nag clan appeared. She relaxed her poise, closed her hood and made room on the rock for her magnificent twin brother!

Oh, he was indeed a wonder to behold! He was easily the most powerful and handsome cobra since his father and grandfather's time. He was nine feet long and as black as the night. He was so black that he shined. But the most distinguishing characteristic he possessed was not the yellow birthmark fang on his lip. No, it was his eyes. One was a very pale blue and the other was hazel. His name was Mee-Kai and he was the son of Nag! This is his story.

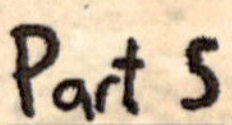

Part 5

MEE-KAI

The egg Nagaena carried into the den in her battle with Rikki Tikki had been thrust into a deep crevice before she turned to fight Rikki. The battle was fierce causing the dirt to soften more along the crevice thereby covering the egg and protecting it from damage.

After the fight was over, an exhausted Rikki noticed the collapse of some walls in the den and had to get out quickly or be buried alive. Seconds after Rikki emerged, the den caved in. Rikki thought about the egg... but never bothered to look for it later and soon forgot it.

Mee-Kai was born in dirt, darkness and starvation. By instinct alone, he managed to overcome all odds and survived. Then he met his sister, Lethalee. She would have killed him had it not been for the yellow fang birthmark. Realizing they were brother and sister, Lethalee repeated the story her uncle told her about the deaths of their parents. It was suspected that the last remaining egg had perished with the cave in but Lethalee had hopes of finding it while retunneling.

She was elated to find her brother had survived and named him Mee-Kai and together, with the help of others, they completed rerouting the tunnels of the den.

Lethalee's utter repulsion for Rikki Tikki tainted Mee-Kai to the point that they had one common goal in mind. They lived for the day Rikki Tikki Tavi would exist no more! And that day was not far off.

Mee-Kai languished beside his sister in all her grandeur and felt proud to be her brother. Not only had she masterminded such a great plan of deceit to those around her, she was able to deceive the main object of their hostility, namely Rikki Tikki Tavi!

However, Mee-Kai had his own personal agenda for loathing Rikki Tikki. After Lethalee told him of his heritage, history and family, Mee-Kai burned with resentment towards Rikki. Alienation from the greatness of the Nag clan by living a life of seclusion: not knowing his roots or family name and history made a permanent scar on Mee-Kai. He did not even know he was living in the very same den of his deceased parents! Had it not been for his sister, he never would have learned about his heritage.

Yes, Mee-Kai had extreme bitterness in his heart for Rikki killing his parents and being born alone. He purposed to get even with Rikki no matter the cost! Yes, Mee-Kai's plans for Rikki were devastating!

After discovering Mee-Kai in the den, Lethalee moved in and taught him how to fight. He grew to love and respect her to the point of adoration! There was none like Lethalee and there was nothing he would not do for her. To be honest, Mee-Kai was a bit afraid of Lethalee. Her intense feelings for Rikki Tikki Tavi unrivaled anything he had ever known! Even his own disdain for Rikki Tikki Tavi paled compared to hers. Mee-Kai felt that his sister would even harm him if he stood in the way of her plans, which is why he kept his own plans of revenge to himself. There was just no telling about Lethalee.

It was just the other day as they lay sunning at the waterfall, that Mee-Kai ventured to ask Lethalee what she would do if someone got to Rikki Tikki before she could exact her revenge upon him. She slowly turned and gazed long and deep into the blue and hazel eyes of her brother. With a hiss, she replied in a low, wicked and cold whisper of a voice, "It would not go well with them". Lethalee's stare was so disturbing that Mee-Kai looked away with a shudder as he crawled off the rock. It was then and there that Mee-Kai decided to leave Rikki to her and the rest to him.

The Continuing Saga of Rikki Tikki Tavi Part 3
Copyright © 2025 by LaDene M. Hayes

ISBN: 979-8894791708 (hc)
ISBN: 979-8894791685 (sc)
ISBN: 979-8894791692 (e)

The Reading Glass Books
1-888-420-3050
www.readingglassbooks.com
fulfillment@readingglassbooks.com